I0532967

Punishing the Art Thief

SHOSHANNA EVERS

Punishing the Art Thief
Shoshanna Evers

Security guard James Tannen feels no shame in blackmailing the beautiful Melissa Dwyer in exchange for his silence, after she crashes a private art unveiling at his employer's house--then costs him his job by stealing a priceless painting that's been missing for decades.

His price? Sexual surrender.

His technique?

Straight out of the BDSM erotic romances Melissa loves to read.

Punishing the Art Thief © 2010 Shoshanna Evers
Original published by Ellora's Cave Publishing, September 2010
Edited by Jillian Bell
Cover art by Rob Sturtz SelfPubBookCovers.com

Print book publication, 2nd edition, © 2013 Shoshanna Evers
Print book publication, 3rd edition, © 2015 Shoshanna Evers

ISBN-10: 0988753790
ISBN-13: 978-0-9887537-9-2

All Rights Reserved.

This is a work of fiction. Any resemblance to persons living or dead or places, events or locations is coincidental.

DEDICATION

For my husband, as always and forever.

CONTENTS

ACKNOWLEDGMENTS

I want to thank God for making me a storyteller! Maybe He didn't have this particular story in mind…but I wouldn't be able to write at all if not for His grace. I love writing about love, in all its crazy forms.

Thank you to my readers. Without you, I would be writing into the abyss. And a special shoutout goes to the Shoshanna Street Team — thank you for your support, and for spreading the word!

Punishing the Art Thief was originally published by Ellora's Cave Publishing in 2010. I'm grateful to them for letting me write all of the dirtiest fantasies that tickled my fancy, and for whipping my stories into shape. Thank you to Jillian Bell, who edited *Punishing the Art Thief*. This was my first published novella, and it led to my career!

It's a thrill to be able to re-issue this novella, three years later, as a self-published book, at a low price for my readers. I'm grateful for the many indie authors who paved the way, showing me a path that has allowed me to be a full-time writer.

Thank you to my cover artist, Rob Sturtz, from SelfPubBookCovers.com for my new cover! I co-founded SelfPubBookCovers.com with Rob to help fulfill my dream of having quality covers at an affordable price available to all indie authors, instantly. If you're a writer, too, you might want to check out the amazing artists we have on board!

Last on the list but first in my heart: thank you, Dear Husband, for being awesome. I love you!

CHAPTER ONE

Melissa Dwyer almost drove past the dark stone mansion — it was set so far back off the road it wasn't visible from her car. The party guests arrived for the fundraiser via a long, winding private drive and left their Mercedes and Porsches for the hired valets. She knew that Westchester County, a half-hour north of Manhattan, had a lot of rich folks. Melissa had just never been invited to mingle with them before.

And she wasn't invited this time, either.

She wore the same long, sea-green satin gown that she wore whenever she crashed a black-tie affair. Her curly brown hair was swept neatly off her lightly made-up face. She looked as if she belonged. As far as Melissa was concerned, she did. She probably loved art a whole lot more than any of these other posers who were just there for the hors d'oeuvres.

Why shouldn't she go to the grand unveiling of Mr. Hamilton's new addition to his personal art gallery? Just because she wasn't able to pay a thousand dollars a head — even if it was for Hamilton's charity du jour — didn't mean she couldn't appreciate the artistic beauty of a good painting.

Mr. Hamilton might be old, but he had excellent taste in contemporary art. The walls of his estate were adorned with a tasteful mix of classic works — originals, Melissa had no doubt — and talented new artists.

There were several men milling about wearing sunglasses and dark suits, talking into radios in hushed tones. Mr. Hamilton had spared no expense to protect his private collection. One of the security guards kept looking over at her.

Do I really stick out so clearly as someone who isn't supposed to be here?

Melissa turned away and tried to blend with the throng of guests heading for the main hall. But the security guard tapped her shoulder.

Melissa nearly jumped out of her skin before arranging an aloof smile on her face and turning to him. *Busted.* Her heart sank with the realization. The worst part was that she had really been looking forward to seeing Mr. Hamilton's new pieces.

"Yes?" she asked.

The security guard smiled. She wasn't expecting that, and the sight of his grin turned the fake, snobby society smile she had put on into a genuine smile. This guy was an intensely good-looking man.

He had dark, closely cropped short hair and olive-colored skin. He looked as if he was about her age — mid-thirties, maybe?

"Sorry," he said. He lowered his sunglasses and looked at her with intense green eyes. "For some reason I thought you looked familiar." The glasses went back up.

She could feel him assessing her beneath his dark glasses and she was suddenly very aware of the fact that he was a…man. Beneath his gaze she felt almost like prey, waiting to be eaten up. A vision of those strong, powerful arms holding her thighs apart as he licked her slowly filled Melissa's mind and she had to turn away before she blushed. She didn't even know his name. She'd have to

2

find out.

"I'm pretty sure I would have remembered you," she said. "I'm Melissa."

"James," he replied.

"As in 'Bond, James Bond'?"

James laughed before shaking his head with his lips closed, as if he suddenly remembered where he was. "James Tannen. It's nice to meet you, Melissa."

Melissa smiled and shook his hand, reveling in how large it was. This guy was huge, and all muscle. His hand enveloped hers and she let her fingers linger for just a moment longer than she knew she should.

"I should go. They're about to begin," she said.

James nodded as she turned to go into the main hall. "Professor Dwyer."

Melissa stopped in her tracks and turned back to look at him, surprised that he really did know who she was.

"I took one of your art history classes a few years ago," James said. "I knew you looked familiar."

Melissa groaned inwardly. She really was busted now. He had to know that as an art history teacher at a community college, she wasn't the type to get invited to this sort of shindig. No teacher she knew would be able to afford a seat at a fundraiser like this.

She looked at him carefully, trying to place his face. She often taught "nontraditional" students who were older than the regular students. They usually were people already working in their chosen careers and looking for some additional mental and academic stimulation by sitting in on her class, or those looking to change jobs. The fact that James was one of those people said a lot about him.

He was so good-looking, his presence so intense, how could she not have recognized him immediately? The sunglasses and the suit must have thrown her, because she certainly remembered him now. He had sat in the back, and he always wore jeans and T-shirts that clung to his muscular torso. She had thought he was handsome back then, too, but he was so large and intimidating looking that she never let herself dwell on her attraction to him.

The party guests around her started moving. If she wanted to stick around to see Mr. Hamilton's new pieces, she didn't have time to reminisce.

"Well, I hope you found the class interesting at least. Nice seeing you." She'd started walking again when she felt his large hand wrap around her upper arm. She didn't want to make a scene so she simply stopped.

"May I see your invitation?"

Melissa tried to laugh but it came out sounding like a croak. "Gosh, I must have given you a bad grade or something."

James let go of her arm, although the warmth where his hand had pressed against her bare skin still lingered. "Actually, I did pretty well." He looked at her and then inclined his head toward the party. "Go ahead."

She tried not to visibly sigh in relief as she hurried toward the main hall, allowing herself to be swallowed up in the crowd of party guests.

* * * * *

Melissa was afraid to stay too long now that she had been recognized. If she wanted to continue to crash private affairs for the chance to see beautiful art that couldn't be found in a public museum, she'd have to leave early and cut her losses.

She stood in the back of the hall and clapped appreciatively when the new artwork was unveiled. It truly was spectacular. The artist was long dead, as was usually the case with pricey works, but his great-grandniece was presenting the piece to the guests and glowing in the collective praise of the group.

Now that Melissa had seen the new art, it was time to get out of there. Unfortunately the single glass of champagne she had drunk had gone right to her bladder. She'd have to find the ladies' room before she could leave if she was going to make the two-hour drive back to

Brooklyn comfortably.

Melissa found the long line to the ladies' room and sighed, trying not to regret that glass of champagne as she crossed her legs. She didn't want to draw attention to herself by requesting to cut the line. She'd just have to find another bathroom.

Excusing herself quietly, Melissa left the line and went back toward the grand foyer, hoping to find a bathroom without a wait.

There was James again… He stood at the foot of the huge main stairway that led to the upper floor, guarding it, she supposed. His muscular arms were crossed in front of his chest.

"James, hi. You wouldn't by any chance know of a bathroom without a wait? It's a bit of an emergency," she said sheepishly.

James raised his eyebrows. "Well, Professor Dwyer."

"Please, call me Melissa."

"Melissa. I suppose you can use one of the bathrooms upstairs, but don't tell anyone I let you up there. It's the third door on the right, I think. Or it might be the fourth. And then," he lowered his voice, "you have to leave. You understand."

"You got it." She wasn't going to waste time pretending that she really had been an invited guest when he obviously had guessed the truth. "Thanks for letting me use the bathroom, you're a lifesaver."

Melissa dashed up the stairs. She knocked on the third door and then opened it, but it wasn't the bathroom. In the dim light Melissa could see a painting hanging in a frame on the opposite wall. Melissa grinned in delight before her bladder reminded her why she was up there to begin with. She backed out of the room and went on to the fourth door. This one was indeed the bathroom.

Melissa relieved herself and then washed her hands, staring at her reflection in the large gilded mirror. What a lucky evening to find one of Mr. Hamilton's private paintings. She knew from some of the other private collections she had seen that many collectors kept their more erotic or exotic pieces in a separate chamber. She'd have to investigate further, just to satisfy her curiosity.

Leaving the bathroom, Melissa peeked into the third door again and stepped inside, flipping on a light that illuminated the single large oil painting. Her jaw dropped. *It couldn't be.*

Could it?

Was this really Rembrandt's only seascape, *The Storm on the Sea of Galilee*? Impossible. It had to be a replica, because that painting had been stolen in 1990 from the Isabella Stewart Gardner Museum. Two men in police uniforms had handcuffed the museum security guards to railings before the staff realized they weren't really cops.

It was the biggest art heist in U.S. history. Those men stole about $300 million worth of paintings — not because they wanted to sell them, or ransom them, but because, Melissa presumed, they wanted to go down in history as having pulled it off.

And the paintings were all still missing.

Melissa crept closer to the painting. The thieves who had stolen the Rembrandt had cut it out of its frame, destroying the outer margins of the canvas. So if she could just see if the edges were cut, she'd know for certain if it was the real deal or a replica. Although it seemed unlikely that a collector like Mr. Hamilton would have a replica at all, much less one hung in what seemed like such a spot of honor.

It had to be the real thing — but she needed to know for sure.

Lifting the frame off the wall, Melissa stumbled under its bulk and weight. The little lamp that underlit the painting was knocked to the floor and smashed. She choked back a gasp of fear as the room fell into shadows once more.

She laid the frame on the hardwood floor, wincing at

the thud it made. *Someone had to have heard that.* She paused. Nothing.

Reaching into her beaded clutch, she pulled out her cell phone and turned it on so that the backlight shone down onto the painting. Feeling like a criminal, she carefully separated the canvas from the frame.

It was real. She was looking at Rembrandt's original stolen painting, knifed edges and all.

She couldn't just leave the painting there. She had to take it home with her so she could figure out how to handle the situation. She'd have to notify the FBI. But how could she leave with a painting without attracting attention?

If she could remove the painting from the frame, it just might be doable. Melissa slid the canvas completely out of the frame and methodically rolled it, setting it aside in the corner as she stepped back and pondered what to do next.

Lifting the now-empty frame, Melissa hung it back on the wall with only the light from her cell phone to guide her, and kicked the shards from the broken light against the wall. In the dark room, it was impossible to tell that anything was amiss. But that wouldn't be the case forever.

What was going to happen when Mr. Hamilton noticed the painting was missing?

She sensed the presence behind her before she heard James' voice. "Just what do you think you're doing, Melissa?"

Melissa turned around, her hands trembling. "James, please, it's not what it looks like."

"Turn around," he said. "Get down on your knees and put your hands behind your head."

"Please, James — "

"Now. Or I'm calling for backup to help restrain you."

Melissa took a shaky breath but she did as he ordered. The long satin gown billowed around her as she kneeled, facing away from him. She could hear him flip the switch and was grateful that she had broken the light, because the fact that the frame on the wall was empty wouldn't be noticed in the dark. Hopefully.

James cursed under his breath, then said, "Mr. Hamilton hired me to make sure that none of his things are stolen. You've been upstairs for way too long. You tricked me."

"I swear, James, I didn't."

"Mrs. Hamilton keeps her diamonds up here. Is that what you were really after?"

Melissa dropped her hands from behind her head in shock. "No."

"How do I know you didn't swipe her jewelry? Why else would you be standing alone in the dark except to smuggle the jewels out of here on your person?"

"You can check," Melissa said, her voice sounding strained and false to her ears. "I don't have anything."

"Oh, I'll check all right. I'm going to search you, and you had better not be lying."

If only she could escape before he figured out she had removed the painting from the frame. But she had to get the Rembrandt in her possession first. It was still rolled in the corner of the room in shadows.

"Stand up," he said. "And put your hands on your head where I can see them."

Melissa stood. She carefully avoided looking at the canvas in the corner or at the empty frame on the wall. From the dim light her cell phone was giving off, she could barely see anything herself. Fear and excitement from being alone with James made her woozy. She would have to do whatever it took to keep all of his attention on her and only her.

As long as he didn't focus on getting the room lit up, she would be home free.

He stepped up behind her, his powerful torso just inches from her back. He methodically ran his hands up the bodice of her gown, running his fingers across the underside of her breasts the way she had seen female

8

prisoners on television get patted down for drugs and needles. He dipped his hand into the top of her gown and carefully fingered the underwire bra she had on.

Did he just caress my nipple? Or am I imagining things?

His hands came down and patted across her hips and down her buttocks, reaching underneath the hem of the satin dress and gliding up her thighs. Melissa moaned involuntarily at the sudden need she felt in her core. She struggled to keep her hands laced on her head, to keep from reaching out and touching him.

He's just doing his job, she reminded herself. Just because she was getting turned-on didn't mean that he was thinking about anything other than his employers' diamonds.

"I don't feel any jewels hidden away under your gown," he said softly. He slipped his hand into her panties. "Or did you hide them deeper?"

Melissa gasped as one long finger run along the crease of her labia, pressing gently against her clit for just a second before he inserted his finger into her pussy. Melissa knew she was wet with need, which was more than a bit embarrassing if James really was just searching her body for stolen jewels.

But she heard James murmur appreciatively as he withdrew his finger and rested his hand against her bare skin under the gown. He pressed his body against hers, holding her back to his chest. Her breath caught in her throat as his massive erection pressed against her lower back.

It seemed as if he was getting just as much out of this impromptu body search as she was.

"See," she said. "I didn't steal anything."

He slid his finger down the crease of her ass and, to her surprise, pushed his finger, already lubricated from her own juices, into her asshole. Her jaw dropped as he withdrew his finger. No one had ever touched her there before.

"I guess not," he said. "But you still need to leave."

Melissa turned around and looked at him, peering into his eyes by the glow of the cell phone light. "You won't tell anyone I was here, right?"

James shook his head. "I think the very thorough body search I just performed proved that you didn't do anything you shouldn't be doing, so there's no reason to mention to Mr. Hamilton that you snuck upstairs."

"You let me upstairs. Right past you."

"No need to mention that either."

Melissa laughed. "Thank you."

She still had to sneak out of there with the Rembrandt. *But how?*

Suddenly the radio on James' hip beeped and a man's voice said through a bit of static, "James, what's your twenty?"

"Get out of here before you get us both into trouble," he said to Melissa as he grabbed the radio. "I can't tell them I'm up here, I gotta be downstairs. Go — now."

Melissa walked toward the door without protest with James right behind her, but as soon as they both were out he turned and walked briskly toward the stairs. Melissa could hear him on the steps as he answered the other man on the radio.

Melissa rushed back into the room before she could talk herself out of it. She went to the corner and picked up the rolled canvas. Holding it reverently in her hands, she lifted her dress and secured the painting against her waist, letting the satin fall back over it.

She took a cautious step. The painting stayed hidden beneath her dress. She crept out of the room, closing the door behind her. The rough canvas scratched against her bare skin.

She wanted to run down the stairs, but the stolen Rembrandt under her dress required that she walk smoothly and slowly.

Someone was going to realize that the painting was missing sooner or later. Probably sooner. And then they would track her down. But since she wasn't actually on the guest list, and the only person who knew she was up there was James, she would be safe as long as James kept his mouth shut. She would just have to be very cautious in the meantime.

Her posture stiff, Melissa stepped out of the mansion and into the night air. Away from James' intoxicating and slightly terrifying presence, she could finally take a deep breath.

That's when it really hit her. She had stolen one of the most famous stolen masterpieces in history. She was a thief of thieves. And now…she actually had Rembrandt's only seascape in her possession!

* * * * *

James tried to control his breathing as he stood guard in the grand foyer by the staircase. He was still slightly out of breath from running like mad to return to his station. Or maybe it was his encounter with Melissa that had taken his breath away.

Melissa. Professor Dwyer. He almost hadn't recognized her in that green dress of hers. She certainly never looked like that when she taught. She looked good then, of course. Just very…professional. Tonight she seemed more open and alive. He couldn't blame her for crashing the party — how could an art buff like her resist?

Just like he couldn't resist flirting with her. And even he had to admit that he'd taken the job of searching her for stolen goods to a new level. Touching her skin, sliding his hands over that lithe little body of hers…he just wished he'd had more time alone with her to explore her properly. He could tie her up in a way that allowed him access to all of her secret places and then he'd —

James coughed and adjusted his body so that his arms, instead of being crossed over his chest, were now covering the front of his slacks, hiding the evidence of his very hard cock. He had to stop thinking of Melissa, at least while he was on the clock. He could think about her later when he was home in Brooklyn.

In fact, he was sure he would.

CHAPTER TWO

Back home in Brooklyn, Melissa stripped out of her green satin dress and carefully hung it up. She'd wear it again when she crashed the charity auction on the Upper West Side. Hopefully she wouldn't get caught at that one.

But if she had to be caught, she couldn't think of anyone she'd rather have doing the catching than James Tannen. That man was just pure, unadulterated walking sex appeal.

She unrolled the canvas carefully and leaned it up against the mirror that sat on top of her dresser. Tomorrow she'd have to go find the perfect frame for it.

Wait, a frame? Really? What I need to do tomorrow is call the FBI and surrender the painting to them.

But she was pretty sure she was going to be framing the Rembrandt instead. How could she give up something so precious?

Melissa lay on her purple bedspread, unable to stop grinning. Looking at the swirls of oil paint on the canvas, she sighed as she lost herself in the intense imagery. Utilizing a rich palette and bold brushstrokes, Rembrandt's command of light and shadow brought to life the scene of Jesus and his disciples battling the ocean. It was a true

13

masterpiece. And it was hers!

The grin fell off her face when a large silhouette darkened her bedroom doorway. Her mouth went dry and she could hear her blood pounding in her ears.

"I'm sorry," she managed to squeak out. "You can have it back. Take it. I won't tell anyone."

The man stepped into her bedroom, the lamplight illuminating his face. "You might not tell anyone, Melissa, but I will."

Melissa jumped up from the bed as she recognized the broad shoulders and the sharp jawline. "James? What the hell are you doing here?"

"Sit the fuck back down."

Melissa sat back on the bed, eyeing James warily. "How—how did you get in here?"

"You don't get to ask the questions, Melissa," he said, his voice dangerously soft.

"Get out!" She tried to put some authority into her voice.

"No," he said simply. "Because I know this painting." His green eyes stared into hers with a ferocity she had never seen in anyone before.

Why in the world had I thought I wanted to get caught by a man like James? He looked as if he was ready to kill her.

Melissa stared back and kept quiet.

"You stole this," he said. It wasn't a question. "I trusted you and you've played me for a fool. You stole this painting from my employer's house, right under my nose. You must think I'm some sort of idiot."

"No, I—"

"You see, I went back upstairs to that room to make sure everything was status quo before I left for the night. I saw the empty frame and I knew it was you. Don't look so shocked that I'm here in your bedroom. You're not that hard to find."

Melissa stood up and walked over toward the painting, keeping her back to the wall like a caged animal. "Did—

did you tell Hamilton? Is he coming after me?"

"Not yet. But he will be. You're a thief. You stole his painting."

"It—it was already stolen," Melissa said.

James looked at her in confusion. "What the hell are you talking about?"

"You don't get it, James. This is a famous painting by a man named Rembrandt—"

"I know who Rembrandt is," he snarled.

"Of course. But this is Rembrandt's *The Storm on the Sea of Galilee*. It was stolen and is—was—still missing. Your employer either hired the men who stole it all those years ago, or he bought it from someone who did. Either way, it's not really his so I didn't really steal it either."

"I don't believe you," James said.

"You don't have to believe me," Melissa sighed. "Just Google it. You'll see."

She gestured toward the closed laptop sitting on her purple bedspread, right next to her book. She winced when she saw what book it was. Would James recognize it as a BDSM title? She truly hoped not. She shook her head. That didn't matter right now. All that mattered was getting James to see the severity of the situation and her innocence.

James sat on the edge of her bed and opened the laptop. It didn't take long before he closed it again and looked at her. "There's an FBI page about it. They're still looking for it."

"That's what I'm telling you."

"You have to give it back, Melissa."

"To who? To you, or to the FBI?"

"Well, if you don't give it back to me, then Mr. Hamilton will figure out it's gone and I'll probably be fired since I was supposed to be guarding the upstairs. But really that painting belongs in a museum, so I suppose for the greater good I'll settle for you handing it over to the FBI."

"And I will. Hand it over to the FBI, I mean. Just not

yet."

"This is serious business. Hamilton will find out eventually, Melissa. And what will happen then?"

"He won't find out it was me, James. I wasn't even on the guest list. I didn't talk to anyone but you. If you don't mention I was there, then no one will ever know I was. And it's not like Hamilton can go to the cops, right? Since it was stolen in the first place?"

"So you're going to turn it in to the FBI?"

"Not exactly. I love this painting. It's like my own personal holy grail. All my life I've been studying art. Looking at masterpieces and delving into the history behind them. This is an actual Rembrandt, and not just any Rembrandt—it's his only seascape."

She paused, unable to put into words exactly what this meant to her—the importance, damn it—so that James could understand.

"And not only is it rare," she added, "it's been missing for two decades. Now that I have it here, I can't just give it up."

James shook his head. "By not turning it over to the FBI so that they can return to it to the museum where it belongs, you are entering into dangerous territory. Whether you like it or not, you've become an art thief."

Melissa prostrated herself before James as he sat on the edge of her bed and looked up into his face imploringly. "I can't lose this painting, James. Please don't turn me in. I'll do anything."

He stood up slowly. He stared down at her from his full height of six foot plus and smiled. "I was hoping you would say that."

Melissa saw the gleam in James' eyes. *What have I just gotten myself into?*

James caressed her face as she kneeled before him on her bedroom carpet, the Rembrandt behind him on the dresser. His hand was large and calloused, but surprisingly gentle.

"I want you to spend the weekend with me," he said.

"Doing what?" she asked nervously.

"Whatever the hell I want, sweetheart."

"Why this weekend? Why not right now?" Melissa reached out her hand and tentatively ran her finger down the bulge in his pants, finding a cock so hard it felt as if it had been chiseled from a slab of marble.

James closed his eyes and inhaled as she reached for his zipper. But he grabbed her wrist, restraining her. "You don't actually think you can keep a stolen Rembrandt in exchange for a blowjob, do you?"

Melissa sighed. That was exactly what she had been thinking.

James took her hand in his and ran it over his cock, still in his pants. "I want this whole weekend with you. Alone. In my bedroom."

"And if I agree to this, then I can keep my painting?"

"Yes."

"You won't tell anyone?" she pressed.

"If anyone asks," James said, removing her hand from his cock, "we'll say it's a well-done replica that you bought at a flea market. And Hamilton won't say anything for fear of being prosecuted himself."

"What's to keep me from just saying that now?"

"To this day," James said, "twenty-plus years after the art heist, there is still an FBI tipline for this painting. I can make the tip online or by phone, any time of day or night. And once I do, you will have the law on your ass. And they will know that it's no replica—just like you knew."

Melissa's gaze flitted to the Rembrandt. She couldn't lose her painting, not now. And she definitely couldn't spend the rest of her life in prison. She stood up slowly. "Okay."

James pulled her up against his muscular chest and kissed her, his lips pressing hard against hers. His kiss took her breath away.

"This is blackmail, you know," she whispered against

his mouth.

"I know." James released her and went over to the pile of books on her bedside table.

Her own personal erotica collection, the books she read with one hand, her other hand buried between her legs as she fantasized about men who looked like…James, actually. Damn, he was good-looking.

James picked up a couple of the books and tucked them under his arm. "Research," he said nonchalantly.

"No," she said. "I don't do those things. I just read about them."

"Not anymore you don't. Be at my house at seven tomorrow night—and plan on sleeping over." He picked a pen off her bedside table and scribbled a nearby Brooklyn address on the bottom of her tissue box. "It's not far from here—we're practically neighbors. See you tomorrow."

* * * * *

James was in a state of shock as he walked back to his house that evening. He couldn't believe that he had really done it—actually broken into Melissa's house and blackmailed her into spending the weekend with him.

And it worked!

He hadn't been truly sure of her intentions with the Rembrandt until she agreed to his offer. This was his one shot, he knew that much. When Melissa was just his art history professor, she had never even given him the time of day, and now she was going to be giving him a whole lot more than that…

He was too jacked up from the adrenaline rush of kissing Melissa to fall asleep. He decided to use the time productively by cleaning his house thoroughly and washing all the linens and towels. Melissa's house had seemed so clean and fresh—he didn't want her thinking he was a slob.

He had one weekend to make her as excited about being with him as he was about being with her. One weekend to make all of her fantasies come true, the ones she said she just read about in her books but never dared to make a reality.

He wished he could call in sick tomorrow so he'd have time to prepare, but he knew he'd have to show up to maintain appearances. He had to be able to defend himself if Hamilton started asking questions about the stolen painting. James would just have to try to get out early if he could—because he had some shopping to do. Toys to buy. And books to read…

* * * * *

Melissa locked her front and back doors and walked back up the stairs, wondering how James had gotten into her house. Strangely enough, the fact that James had tracked her down so quickly didn't upset her. Maybe that was just because she found herself irresistibly attracted to him. They had never really spoken before their encounter at Hamilton's party. She wasn't sure he had ever even raised his hand in class.

And now she was spending the weekend with him.

She stood in front of her Rembrandt, imagining herself on that fated boat the painting depicted as it was tossed by the roiling sea.

Worth it. Totally worth it. She could handle anything for forty-eight hours, right? One weekend with him doing, as he said, "whatever the hell he wanted", and then she would be free. Free to live her life with a very special piece of priceless art on her bedroom wall, and free from James…not that she was sure she even wanted to be free of him.

Melissa turned off the light and crawled under her purple bedspread. What about those erotic books he had stolen from her bedside table? He had called it research…but when Melissa thought about the sorts of things that were in those books, God… it made her blush.

She didn't know why, but she just really got off on reading about certain things. Reading and reading only. She had never tried any of the risqué sexual techniques that she read about and masturbated to. Bondage. Nipple clamps. Vibrators. Butt plugs. Spanking. Whipping.

What exactly did James have in store for her? If he was using her personal book collection as a script, she was in for a wild ride indeed.

She couldn't do this. Shouldn't do this. She should go to the police herself. Turn herself in. Give back the stolen Rembrandt. She shouldn't willingly show up on James' doorstep for a weekend at his mercy.

But she knew that she would. Because for some strange reason, she really wanted to.

CHAPTER THREE

The following day, James didn't even get a chance to go to work. One of Hamilton's men called him and told him he was fired effective immediately. No reason was given, but why would there be? He was done as a private security guard. He'd have to find something new before he burned through his savings.

James would have been a lot more upset about it if he didn't have the enticing distraction that Melissa's weekend stay was going to provide.

Hanging up his black suit in the closet, James threw on some jeans, poured a cup of coffee, and spent the morning reading through the books he had borrowed from Melissa's impressive erotica collection. The corners were turned down on certain pages, and he spent extra time on those sections.

He pulled out a scrap of paper so he could compile a list of special items he would need to buy that afternoon. His cock hardened as he imagined using silk ropes to tie her up, spanking her with his bare hand, perhaps using a belt on her if she was very naughty…

Well, she had a stolen priceless painting in her bedroom. She was definitely very naughty. And he knew he was going to enjoy punishing her thoroughly.

He wondered if she had ever been fucked in the ass. Probably not. He'd never even heard her talk about a boyfriend before, in those moments he had overheard her chatting with the adults taking her class. Never seen her whisper on her cell phone with a lover between classes. He would buy an anal plug for her and break her in slowly.

But not too slowly. She was, after all, going to be here for punishment.

He knew that was what she wanted. It had to be — otherwise her erotic books would be a bit more varied. Instead, all of the dog-eared pages were solely about being dominated. Tied up. Forced to orgasm again and again to please her Master — which this weekend, would be him.

He couldn't believe his luck. All this time he had been fantasizing about throwing his art history professor over his shoulder and running away with her — tying her up, having his way with her — she'd been fantasizing about those things too. It was too perfect.

He'd never met a woman before who shared his desires. The last date he'd tried to spank had slapped him across the face and walked out the door. The one time he had suggested bondage to a lover, she had wanted to tie *him* up. Most women just weren't on the same page as him.

James grinned as he flipped through the pages of Melissa's books. Well, his little art thief was definitely on the same page as he was. Like this page with the whip.

James realized he was stroking his cock and abruptly stopped himself. She was going to be showing up at his doorstep at seven o'clock sharp, and he wanted to be ready for her. He was going to save all of his sexual energy for Melissa, not waste it on masturbation.

He pulled his coat on and grabbed his car keys. He had shopping to do.

* * * * *

At seven o'clock, Melissa took a deep breath and rang the doorbell of James' large brownstone. He opened the door and greeted her with a smile.

"Glad you could make it," he said as he stepped aside so she could enter.

Melissa nodded and dropped her overnight bag on the floor in the front hall. She hoped he didn't notice that her hands were trembling. He was dressed in jeans and a black T-shirt that hugged his body, showing off his broad shoulders and impressive biceps. She hadn't been sure what to wear, so she'd opted for a casual, short, flouncy skirt and a tank top.

"Nice place," she said.

James shrugged. "It was my grandparents'. I couldn't afford a place like this otherwise." He smiled. "You look really good," he said, taking her hand.

"Um, thanks. You too."

James laughed. "That's very kind of you, Melissa. But flattery won't keep me from punishing you for that Rembrandt."

What did he have in mind?

"Punishment, huh?" she asked as she sat down on the couch next to him. "I never took you for the kinky type."

"No, you never took me for any type at all, I imagine," he said smoothly. "But that's going to change right now. Bend over my knee."

Melissa stared at him blankly. "Are you serious?"

"As a heart attack."

"I've never done this before," she said, laughing nervously.

"You were never spanked as a child even?" James asked.

"No, my parents were into time-outs. But let's not talk about parents. Kinda kills the mood."

"Good point," James said. "The time for talking is over."

He took her upper arms firmly in his large hands, pulled her over his lap and held her there, but she wasn't struggling. She couldn't believe she had let herself get into this position — both literally across James' lap, and the whole situation — being blackmailed over a stolen painting.

But not just any stolen painting. A Rembrandt. *The* Rembrandt. She felt James' hand run down her skirt and caress her ass. He lifted her skirt up.

"You have a gorgeous ass," he said, "but these panties won't do." He tugged her boy shorts off, removing her high heels and letting them drop to the hardwood floor. "I bought you a thong."

He dangled a piece of flimsy black spandex fabric in front of her eyes before she felt him sliding the thong up her legs.

"I never wear thongs," she said. "They feel like I'm walking around with a wedgie all day."

James laughed and snapped the spandex into place, caressing her still-bare buttocks. "Well, you're wearing a thong this weekend."

And with that proclamation, he smacked his hand down across one of her ass cheeks, then the other. She gasped. She still couldn't believe she was doing this.

Smack!

Then again and again, until her buttocks become warm with the sting.

"Hey!" she cried out as he slapped her especially hard.

Immediately, he stopped. He pulled her skirt down and lifted her up off his lap. "We need to get something straight, Melissa. You are here because you want to be. Because you are, in essence, prostituting yourself for the right to keep a painting that doesn't belong to you."

Melissa could feel herself blush. "I'm not a prostitute. I'm an art history teacher!"

James ignored her. "We had an agreement. A contract, if you will. You are mine to do with as I please for the weekend. And I will never tell a soul about the Rembrandt in your bedroom. I won't turn you in."

"I know — I just, I can't be spanked like a child…"

James smiled wryly. "May I?" he asked as he reached his hand under her skirt. He slipped a finger beneath the tight thong that was soaked with wetness he had evoked in her. "Your pussy tells a different story, Melissa."

Embarrassed, Melissa averted her eyes as he removed his hand.

"Your pussy is telling me not to listen to what you say," he whispered. "Because you're saying you don't want this, and you're lying."

She could feel his eyes on her as she stared at her boy-short panties lying on the floor at his feet. *Damn him.* He was right. She did want this.

She'd been looking forward to this evening — with a mix of trepidation and excitement — since he had propositioned her last night. The whole idea of giving up control turned her on…and scared the hell out of her.

"How about this," James said, and she finally looked up into his intense green eyes. "If you ever change your mind, you can just say our safeword, and I will stop everything, and you will go home. Of course, then I'll turn you in."

"Why are you doing this, James?"

"Because I've wanted to have you since I first saw you. And because you want me too — or else you wouldn't be here."

Melissa took in a shaky breath. She was going to go through with this, even though she was scared. She was also turned-on. "What's the safeword?"

James grinned. "Rembrandt."

* * * * *

James pulled her onto his lap so that she straddled him, and kissed her, letting his tongue enter her mouth, tasting her. She smelled delicious, as if she had just the tiniest drop of floral perfume on.

He fingered one of the curly tendrils of hair that fell against her shoulder, trailed his tongue down the curve of her neck and kissed the hollow of her throat, her pulse fluttering rapidly beneath his lips.

Having her here was worth being fired. He still hadn't told her what had happened with that. No point in spoiling the mood.

He pulled her tank top down so that her bra was visible. She was wearing a red lacy bra that looked like it hadn't been worn very often. He smiled appreciatively. Could she have worn it to impress him? This was a woman who was used to having the upper hand. The careful, organized professor. She probably had to be in control of everything.

But not this weekend. This weekend he was in charge.

He pulled one of her breasts up and out of the bra, running his fingers softly over her nipple before pinching it. She gasped as it hardened and he kissed it, rolling his tongue around her areola before sucking the whole nipple into his mouth.

She moaned as he took her other breast out of its confines and tweaked that peak with his fingers as well.

"You like that, do you?" he asked, the hard tip still in his mouth. "How about this?" He flicked her nipple with his tongue, then lifted his mouth from her breast to roll both tight buds between his fingers. "I've got a toy for these little nipples for later."

Melissa's eyes widened. James dipped his hand underneath her skirt again and ran his fingers under the thong and along her wet cunt. She was practically dripping. She arched her body forward, trying to press her clit against his finger, but he wasn't ready to give Melissa her release. Not yet.

He yanked the spandex thong in an upward motion, snapping it against her clit. She moaned and stopped trying to press her clit against him.

"I wasn't done spanking you, you know," he said.

She bent over his knee immediately, without him even having to ask her. "Sorry," she said, but she didn't sound sorry.

He smacked her ass twice for good measure before standing up, pulling her with him.

She started to adjust her thong but he stopped her with a hand gesture. "Leave it," he said. "I like knowing it's riding up your pussy lips and your ass crack."

"It's uncomfortable," she said, pulling the thong down.

"I think you're trying to give me a reason to punish you."

"No I'm not! I mean, I didn't mean to."

James took one of the ropes that he had bought earlier that day and held it up. "I've been reading your books," he said as he pulled up her skirt.

He wrapped the rope around her waist and brought it up through her legs, over the thong. Stopping momentarily, he tied a knot in the part of the rope that would press against her clit. Then he pulled the rope tight.

Melissa raised her eyebrows as if wondering what he was up to. James smiled. She'd see soon enough.

He tied the rope in an intricate knot at the base of her spine, where she would not be able to undo it herself without a great deal of difficulty.

"Pull your skirt down," he said.

Melissa obeyed, her hands fidgeting at her sides as she seemed to struggle to not attempt to release her bonds.

"Walk over to the edge of the couch and bend over for me," he commanded. She gasped as she started walking.

"How's that feel?" he asked, genuinely curious. He could only imagine what it must feel like to have a rope pressing against her clit, the knot rubbing insistently against her with each step she took.

"It's — it's uncomfortable — but it feels good too — does that make sense?" she asked. "It's worse when I walk. I mean, it makes that knot rub my clit more then."

"Good," he said. "Bend over the arm of the couch and lift that skirt again."

She did as he asked but she looked back over her shoulder at him nervously. "What are you going to do?"

"I'm going to paddle you," James said. "That way I can make your ass as red and sore as I like without hurting my hand."

* * * * *

"I don't want you to paddle me," she said, her eyes wide with fright as he brandished the wooden paddle.

It looked very, very hard. Melissa felt the handle of the paddle nudge her legs open wide, and the rope he had tied over her mound pressed against her clit even more.

He slid his hand under the rope, under her thong, and caressed her pussy. She knew her body had betrayed her again — she was wet and ready for whatever he wanted to give her. And not just because she wanted to keep her stolen painting.

James laughed as she bucked her pussy against his hand, and withdrew his fingers before she could make herself come.

"You're going to come tonight," he promised her as the paddle slammed against her ass, causing her to yelp with the sudden sting of it. "But I'm in control of your orgasms now. Not you. Surrender to me, Melissa."

He brought the paddle down again, hard, reddening both of her ass cheeks at once.

She cried out but she didn't beg him to stop. She didn't want him to stop. And he didn't. Her skin burned and her eyes watered as he rained down the blows, showing her no mercy.

Then he dropped the paddle to the living room floor and she felt his lips press against her burning buttocks, kissing her. "Let's go upstairs," he said.

Melissa hoped that once she was in his bedroom he would finally allow her to come. She stood up on trembling legs, her skirt covering the rope that was tied to stimulate her pussy so expertly she had to wonder where James had learned the skill.

Each step up the stairs rubbed the rope against her clit some more, until she was practically panting with need by the time James led her to his king-sized, four-poster bed.

He had several paintings hanging on the walls. They were intriguing — the paintings were of a woman in various states of bondage. They looked to be a series by the same artist. She could see why he kept them hidden away in his bedroom, considering the subject matter, but it seemed a shame that more people wouldn't see them. They were quite good.

"This is a talented artist," she said. "But I've never seen his work before."

James smiled. "I imagine no one has."

He turned her around and untied the rope between her legs. Melissa touched her pussy tentatively.

"I'm going to tie you to my bed and, with your permission, I'd like to gag you," he said.

"With my permission?" Melissa asked. "Why start asking for that now?"

"Because once I gag you, you won't have the option of saying the safeword. You have to give me your consent ahead of time. Like right now."

"What are you going to do to me?"

"Nothing that would cause you any harm. I just want to act out a scene from one of your erotica books."

"Which scene?"

"I won't tell you exactly which one — but it's from one of your dog-eared pages, so I know that it's one of your favorite go-to scenarios to read about when you play with yourself," he said, smiling lazily.

Melissa tried to think of all of the special pages she had dog-eared, and all of the different things that she loved to read about but never had the courage to actually try out in real life. She knew if he told her which fantasy he was going to bring to reality for her fear would keep her from doing it. She wanted to have her fantasies become a reality, though — even if it was just for one weekend.

James took her chin in his hand and looked at her. "I — I've always been fascinated by you, Melissa. Since I sat in on your class. I think you are so special. I feel like I'm falling in love with you. And…you're safe with me."

Melissa's mouth opened in shock. *Did he just say that he was falling in love with me?*

"You can't love me," she protested.

James shook his head. "Too soon to tell you, I know. I can understand why you don't believe it's true. But it is. So you're safe with me."

Melissa nodded mutely. She lay down on the bed and looked up at James' handsome face. She trusted him. Something about him — he was pushing all of her buttons, but that was okay. He was right. She needed to give up control once in a while.

"Take your clothes off," he whispered.

She obeyed, nearly ripping her tank top in an effort to get naked quickly.

He took her arm and tied a rope around her wrist. He pulled it taut, tying the other end to one corner of the four-poster bed. He did the same to her other arm. When he put the gag on her — a leather-covered bar that ran between her teeth, allowing her to breathe through her mouth but muffling her words and her volume —her pussy throbbed.

"This," he said as he strapped her to the sides of a horizontal wooden pole with ankle restraints on either end, "is a spreader bar. It will keep you from closing those pretty legs of yours."

"And now," he said as sat down on the bed beside her, "you're going to have your orgasm."

He ran his fingers over her clit, circling it gently as she moaned beneath her gag. His fingers felt so amazing, but it wasn't enough. She pressed her hips up, trying to increase the contact with her clit.

"Naughty little pussy," he said, and slapped her clit with his fingers.

The gag muffled her gasp as he slowly started playing with her again, running a finger along her dripping labia and dipping it inside her pussy before slapping her pussy lips once more. She groaned, imploring him with her eyes to let her come.

"You want to come, don't you, Melissa?" he said.

She nodded her head vigorously.

"Will you have as many orgasms as I want you to?"

She nodded her head again, desperate for release. *Of course I'll have as many orgasms as he wants!*

James stood up from the bed, walked over to his dresser and took something out. Melissa lifted her head, straining to see what he was up to. He opened a package to reveal a large vibrator.

With the toy still off, he pressed the head of the wand directly against her clit. The pressure of the hard rubber against her swollen little nub was almost enough to send her over the edge — and it wasn't even turned on yet.

Taking a long piece of rope, he expertly tied the vibrator in place, wrapping the rope around her thighs and hips to secure it to her clit.

"Wiggle for me, see if you can dislodge this," he ordered.

Melissa obeyed. The vibrator stayed pressed against her, even when she swiveled her hips. That thing wasn't going anywhere and, she realized as she pulled on her wrist restraints, neither was she. She tried to close her legs only to be reminded of the spreader bar forcing them wide open. She was helpless and trapped.

And then he turned the vibrator on.

She was so ready for him, so ready to come — her orgasm hit a crescendo immediately, and she cried out against her gag as she came within seconds. She looked at him, a satisfied smile on her gagged lips. But James stayed standing on the other side of the bedroom, watching her.

And the vibrator continued to buzz against her overstimulated clit.

She tried to ask him to untie her, to release her, but her words were muffled by the gag.

"I'm not letting you go so easily, Melissa," he said. "You said you'd have as many orgasms as I wanted to give you. And I want to give you a couple more than you had in mind."

Another wave of sensation threatened to overtake her senses as the vibrator tied to her pussy forced her to climax again. Her moans were soft against the gag.

And just like that, she knew which scene he was going to reenact for her...

"Do you remember this scene, Melissa? Do you remember what happened here?"

She nodded her head weakly. In one of her favorite erotica books — the one she used most often to get in the mood to come — she had dog-eared the page on a scene that she found exquisitely sexually exciting. The heroine had been caught secretly masturbating with her vibrator, despite her Master's explicit wish that she save her orgasms for when he gave them to her. As her punishment, her Master tied her up so she was unable to escape. Then he left her alone with a vibrator tied to her pussy.

It didn't take long before the toy that was once her friend, giving her orgasms that she so desperately craved, became her enemy — torturing her clit with its constant hard vibrations. And the heroine had to endure this sexual pussy torture until her Master deemed her appropriately chastised.

Melissa moaned as the vibrator buzzed mercilessly. She pressed her ass — still sore from the paddle — back against the bed as if she could get away from it. But there was no escape. She wondered at what point pleasure became pain — and she wondered if she even cared.

She wanted to be released — the tears that rolled down her cheeks unbidden were proof — but her soaking-wet pussy and the electrifyingly intense orgasm that ripped through her were proof that she wanted to be dominated by James even more.

She caught his gaze from across the room as he stood watching her thoughtfully, his cock fully erect in his jeans. She cried out against her gag, begging to be freed.

"I don't think you quite get that I'm in charge this weekend," he said, not moving from his position. "I'm going to give you some more time alone to think about that before I release you."

And he left the room.

CHAPTER FOUR

James stood at the doorway listening to Melissa's stifled moans as she lay bound on his bed with his vibrating wand strapped tight against her clit.

He could have kicked himself for admitting that he was falling for her. He probably sounded desperate. She didn't even believe him. But it was true — and had been for a while. Ever since he had taken her art history class, Melissa's image came to his mind whenever he looked at amazing art — and whenever he masturbated. Melissa probably thought he was just professing his feelings as a way to get her to agree to play along, but he had no intentions of manipulating her like that.

He wanted her to be here because she wanted to be here.

James knew that for Melissa, the blackmail about the painting had become a way to give herself permission to do what she already wanted to do. She wanted to have her fantasies played out for her — whether she was willing to admit it or not.

Still, he shouldn't have slipped up like that by telling her how he felt about her. James sighed and pushed back into the bedroom to release Melissa from her orgasm torture. They had all weekend to play.

She lay, panting on the bed, a sheen of perspiration covering her gorgeous naked body. James walked over to her, unzipped his jeans, and pulled out his cock. It was so hard it was almost painful. He stroked it, watching her eyes as she came again, hard.

Stroking himself faster, he ejaculated, a low grunt escaping his lips as the white jet spurted onto her flat stomach and pooled in her bellybutton. James waited another moment while he caught his breath, then he turned off the vibrator and ungagged her.

"Thank you," she said, breathless. "I thought you were going to leave me like that all night."

James smiled as he gently untied her. "I thought you might be more comfortable if you could sleep snuggled under the covers with me."

She touched her pussy tentatively. Her clit was so swollen it had popped out of its hood.

"How's that feel?" he asked.

Melissa shook her head and laughed. "Ouch. In a good way. It aches in a strange...delicious way."

"And your legs?"

Melissa smiled and stretched like a cat on the bed. "A little stiff — but it was worth it. I love the feeling of being tied up so securely."

"You rest there so I can clean you up," he said.

He went into the bathroom and got a wet washcloth. She had no idea how amazing she was. Walking back over to her, he carefully wiped his seed from her belly.

Looking up at him, Melissa asked, "Are we going to fuck?"

"Don't be crude, Melissa," he said. "It's our first date. I'm not easy, you know."

Melissa laughed as James dropped down onto the bed next to her, pulling the sheets over them. She ran her fingers over his T-shirt and kissed his lips.

"I've always been so turned-on by the forced orgasm

fantasy," she murmured, her face close to his. "The reality of it was a little harder to bear than just reading about it though."

"There are so many things I can do to punish that little swollen pussy of yours," James said as he lay next to her, his body pressed against her back, spooning her. "But tonight I've put you through enough. We've got all weekend."

Melissa made a small sighing sound as she nestled against him, and they fell asleep in each other's arms.

* * * * *

Melissa woke before James did the following morning. Looking at the digital alarm clock, she realized it was actually the afternoon. When she slid out of his embrace, he rolled over, still sleeping. She took her overnight bag with her into the bathroom.

Standing in the shower, Melissa let the hot water rain down on her back as she washed her hair. Last night had been intense. Right now, the sun was shining outside and the things they had done in the dark seemed crazy to her in the light of day. Bending over James' lap while he spanked her, letting him tie her up and force her to multiple orgasms, was all a part of the emotional and physical surrender he had demanded of her. And amazingly, she had given in easily. She had wanted to.

Melissa shook her head to clear her thoughts as she stepped out of the shower.

There was a knock on the bathroom door.

Melissa smiled. "Come in." She didn't bother to wrap herself in the towel, preferring to stand on the plush bath rug dripping wet.

James opened the door and grinned sleepily at her, his dark hair ruffled from the pillow.

"What a beautiful sight to wake up to," he said as he wrapped his arms around her naked body.

"I'm getting you all wet," she said.

"Don't care," he said, dropping his head and licking the

water droplets trickling between her breasts. She felt his erection poking into her belly through his flannel sleep pants.

"I feel bad I didn't get a chance to pleasure you last night," she said. "You gave me orgasm after orgasm."

"That's okay," he said, moving his mouth to her nipple and eliciting a gasp from her as he pulled on it gently with his teeth.

"No, it's not okay," she insisted. "I want you to feel some of what you gave me last night." She pressed her hands against the front of his pants and his cock jumped under her fingers.

He watched, not moving, as she pulled his pants down around his ankles and fell to her knees in front of him. "Get up," he ordered.

"But I want to — " she started to protest.

"Trust me, I want you to suck my cock too. I just want to move the game into the shower."

He peeled off his shirt and kicked the flannel pants off his ankles and turned the shower on, standing under the hot stream of water. "Come in, the water's fine."

Melissa stepped into the tub in front of him, feeling the mist from the showerhead spraying over James' body as it splashed on her.

James grabbed a bar of soap and handed it to her. "Wash me."

Melissa took the soap and ran it across his abdomen, trailing it lower, letting her lathered hands caress his member slowly. She cupped his balls, gently washing them as James took the soap from her and quickly lathered up his chest, underarms, and finally his ass crack. He turned in the water, letting the shower rinse him thoroughly.

Letting the lather build up again, he traced his hand down her ass. She stiffened as she felt his finger stop at her anus.

"Please," she whispered, but she wasn't sure what she was pleading for.

She remembered how he had slid his finger in her ass when he was searching her for stolen diamonds. She had been so surprised that there had been no time to protest. Now, as he lazily stroked the cleft of her buttocks, she tensed in anticipation.

"I want you clean, inside and out," he said as he slid one soapy finger into her ass up to the knuckle.

She cried out at the sudden invasion but James just laughed.

"Oh, come on," he said. "This is nothing. Wait till you see the size of the butt plug I got for you."

Melissa's eyes widened. "No way," she said.

James wiggled his finger inside her before withdrawing it and rinsing the soap from his hand under the shower stream.

She wondered if she would still find it easy to submit to him now that he was asking her to do something that she was truly afraid of doing. She had never even had a finger up there before he had strip-searched her — not even when she masturbated.

Sure, she liked reading about it. But that was just because she liked reading about women doing whatever their Masters ordered. And for some reason, most men had a thing for anal sex. Maybe it was because they liked the idea of doing something taboo. Or maybe they liked how tight a little anus was compared to a vagina that could, if needed, stretch to birth a child. Or maybe they liked the moans of pain that a hard ass fucking was sure to induce…

"I read all about your fantasy in your naughty books, Melissa. You can't deny that it turns you on."

"Reading about it, maybe, but — " she sputtered.

"Don't you want to please me?" he asked. His question sounded sincere.

Melissa didn't even have to think about it. "Yes, I do."

She had always fantasized about being with a man like James, and she had always fantasized about being dominated. Suddenly, she was getting both of her fantasies at once. It was a little overwhelming. The fact that he was still holding the stolen Rembrandt over her head didn't even matter to her anymore.

She'd do what he said just because it was James saying it. Her James.

He gently placed his hands on her shoulders and guided her down to a kneeling position. The porcelain tub hurt her knees but she didn't care. She had been dreaming about his cock all night. He was hard and huge.

She wrapped her hand around the base of his erection and pressed her lips against the head, twirling her tongue around it. A bead of clear salty fluid formed at the tip of his cock, but when she opened her mouth to take in more of him the water from the shower got in her mouth and washed his taste away.

Sucking hungrily, she licked the underside of his cock as he wrapped his hand in her hair, holding her face against him, her mouth impaled on his length. She slid her hand up and down his shaft, working just the first couple of inches with her mouth.

"Drop your hands," he said. "I want you to take all of me in your mouth."

She dropped her hands and started slowly swallowing his cock. The water dripped over her face and suddenly she felt as if she were being suffocated.

"I can't, it's too much — " she started to say, but the moment her mouth opened James seized the opportunity to thrust far past her lips, sliding his entire length down her throat as he held her hair tightly in his fist.

Melissa moaned as he pounded away at her mouth.

"Touch yourself," he said, and Melissa buried her hand in her pussy as the hot jet of his cum shoot down her throat.

He was so far back in her throat, past her tongue, that she couldn't even taste it. He released her hair and her head flew back, a stream of warm water from the shower running into her open mouth before he pulled her to stand.

Her pussy was aching, pulsing with need as he turned off the shower and wrapped her in a large, clean towel. She hadn't had time to reach an orgasm.

She started to grab for her clothes but James stopped her with a gesture.

"I like you naked," he said.

Melissa blushed. "Will you make me come too?"

"I only want you to come when I make you come," he said. "Or if I order you to reach an orgasm for me. But unless I tell you to, you shouldn't masturbate."

"Ever?"

Why did I ask that? Why am I asking about forever?

"I promise I'll keep you more than satisfied. If you're good, of course."

Melissa felt the moisture pooling between her legs as she nodded. She wanted to be good.

"Come on," he said, leading her back to the bed.

He pulled a large pillow shaped like a ramp out from under the bed and tossed it on top of the comforter next to Melissa. It was covered in a soft black microfiber and red fuzzy straps, about three inches wide, were attached by clips on each end.

"Lean over this," he said, laying her body so that her ass was up in the air, her knees resting on the bed and her body and arms pressed against the down slope of the ramp.

She heard the scratchy sound of Velcro as he secured each of her wrists in the soft, fuzzy cuffs. Wider straps held her thighs in place against the side of the ramp. Her clit pressed against the edge, throbbing with desire.

He gave her a playful smack on the ass and Melissa jumped, instinctively trying to move away from his hard hand. She didn't go anywhere.

James laughed. "Trying to get away?"

He spanked her again, and as she ground her pussy into

the pillow, desperate for more contact, his hand suddenly switch position and slap upward onto her pussy lips. She squealed in surprise and gave up trying to cheat herself to an orgasm.

"There's nowhere to go, silly girl."

"Please, make me come," she begged.

Her legs trembled as she he slapped her pussy lips again, his fingers spreading her labia wide so her clit was exposed. The next slap landed directly on her clit and she nearly screamed with the painful pleasure of it.

"We're just getting started," he said.

* * * * *

James looked at Melissa bound to his sex ramp pillow and his cock came to life again. Her ass was creamy white except for the little pink blotches he had created with his light spanking.

He went to his dresser and took out the butt plug that he had bought just for Melissa's virgin ass. It was relatively small, just a little over four inches long, with a tapered end that spread to a one-and-one-fourth-inch-wide head, and then it narrowed again before a second, larger bulb came up below it. It was designed so that her anus could close around the narrow part following the bulb. The base was wide so it couldn't get lost inside her. He knew the second bulb was a bit big for a beginner like Melissa, but he wanted to challenge her a little.

She gasped as he spread a dollop of lube over her anus.

"James," she said breathlessly, "I'm scared it might hurt."

"Well," he said, as he spread even more lube over the length of the butt plug in his hand, "it might hurt going in. Probably will. But once it's in, it should provide a really nice, filling sensation."

He pressed the head of the plug against her tiny pink asshole, pushing gently, stopping to smack her butt cheek when he saw she was moving her hips forward in an effort to get away from the invading plug.

"That's not going to work, sweetheart," he said. "This is going in your ass whether you like it or not."

Melissa moaned.

"But you do like it, don't you?" James asked, sliding a finger into her pussy.

It was dripping. He pressed the plug in harder and she gasped again as the first bulb stretched her asshole open wide before it snapped shut around the narrow portion of the plug like a hungry little mouth closing. She was moaning again but she was also nodding her head. Yes, she liked it.

"You're not done yet, Melissa. There's a wider portion now. Relax. Breathe in."

As he heard Melissa breathe in slowly, he pushed the second, wider bulb into her ass, loving the sight of her asshole opening wide as Melissa made soft whimpering noises. It was all the way inside her now, the rectangular base hidden between her butt cheeks.

He spanked her again just to watch the muscles contract around the hard plug inside her.

"Good job," he said as he loosened her restraints.

She sat up, her face flushed. She reached around as if to remove the plug but James grabbed her hand. "I don't think so."

"But — can't I take it out?"

"Sure, just not yet. We're going out for lunch first."

"You can't seriously expect me to wear this out in public, can you?"

"Just put some jeans on. No one will see it. But it will help stretch you out."

"I won't do it," she said.

He laughed. "You're testing me again. Okay, if you don't want to go out wearing the plug, then you can stay here — but I'm going to tie you back up, and that little plug is going to be replaced by this." He walked over to his dresser and pulled out a plug that was easily twice as long as the one she was wearing — and not only was the head bulbous and wide, it tapered out to a width the size of her fist. "That little toy you have in you now is nothing compared to this monster."

Melissa's eyes widened. "Okay, I'll get dressed."

The first challenge, Melissa realized, was sitting down in the car. The plug nudged her and she wriggled in her seat. It was definitely a strange sensation.

When they got to the diner, Melissa felt so awkward following James to their table, she wondered if anyone could notice her walking funny. The plug felt like it was falling out a bit.

The hostess asked James if they wanted a booth or a table. She didn't realize why he requested a table until they sat down, and Melissa cried out softly as the hard wood pressed against her sore, spank-reddened buttocks and pushed the plug back into her ass. James smiled.

"You should really learn how to curb your vocal displays in public," James said. "Especially if I'm going to keep your ass freshly spanked every day."

Melissa felt butterflies in her stomach at his words. *What did he mean every day?*

She was only supposed to be his for the weekend — but did he want to keep seeing her? She hoped so. Something about James fit her so well. No other man had made her feel the way that he did. She had never felt comfortable telling previous lovers about her true, hidden fantasies — she was afraid they would think she was a freak. But James was even kinkier than she was.

"Stand up," James said.

She stood.

"Now," he said, "I want you to sit down, hard, and don't make the slightest grimace."

Melissa did as she was told, feeling like her ass was on fire. A little moan escaped her despite her closed lips.

"We'll have to work on that," James muttered as he picked up his menu. "What do you want to eat?"

The rest of the meal passed in a pleasurable blur. They

ate and laughed and generally just enjoyed each other's company. They had a lot in common in addition to the fact that they really clicked in the bedroom.

James was a huge fan of art, which made Melissa happy. Melissa was so into the conversation that she even found herself forgetting she was wearing the butt plug. Well, she could forget until she shifted position in her chair, at which point she would be abruptly reminded. And she found herself shifting in her chair quite a bit since the spankings he had given her had left her with a sore ass.

When they had finished eating, James picked up the bill and they drove back in companionable silence.

"What's next?" Melissa asked as they pulled up in front of his house.

James smiled. "You'll see."

* * * * *

Melissa was bound on his bed, her wrists tied to her knees and her knees spread lewdly open with the spreader bar. James hadn't let her remove the butt plug yet, and as she squirmed, testing the strength of her bindings, it nudged her deep inside.

She could feel herself getting wet as she watched James get something out of his dresser drawer and walk over to her. Would he force orgasm after orgasm on her again? She half hoped so.

But it wasn't a vibrator that James came up to her with. He was holding something silver in his hands, with a delicate chain. It almost looked like jewelry.

"Nipple clamps," he said as he attached one firmly to her already erect nipple.

Melissa gasped as the sensation hit her. When James attached the second nipple clamp, the thin silver chain hung between her breasts like a necklace, tickling her and moving ever so slightly as she breathed.

"You look so beautiful like that," he said thoughtfully.

"Please, please fuck me," Melissa said. "I've been wanting your cock in me since we met at Hamilton's party."

James smiled. "But we didn't meet at Hamilton's party. You just can't remember me from your class — but I certainly remember you. I've thought about you, fantasized about you, for a very long time. Since I first heard you speak about art history."

"We've wasted years then. I wish you had the balls to ask me out back then," she said boldly.

He laughed. "Now that you've ascertained that I've got the balls, what do you intend to do with them?"

"Whatever you want me to."

James smiled as he gently tugged the chain between her nipple clamps. "Good answer."

Her breath drew in for a moment as one of the nipple clamps slid a bit, creating a new wave of sensation in her hard left nipple. "So what took you so long?"

"I had to get you where I wanted you."

"And where's that?" Melissa asked.

"In my bed, tied up just for me, so I could do whatever I wanted to your helpless body. Just like this. But right now, I just want to look at you. To capture this moment."

James leaned back against his dresser and picked up what appeared to be a sketchpad, and a pencil. His handsome face assessed her carefully, and then he turned back to his paper, sketching her likeness.

Melissa felt a surge of warmth in her face and she knew she was blushing. To be drawn in such a provocative position... She looked around her at the paintings on the wall in James' room and the realization dawned on her.

"You painted these."

James nodded, lifting his head from his sketchpad briefly to study her before putting his pencil to the paper once more. "You may not have noticed, because I didn't even realize it myself until this weekend. But these paintings — I would create them when I was fantasizing. And when I fantasized the woman always had your face, your demeanor."

46

"What are you saying?" Melissa asked softly.

"The women in my paintings…they're all you."

Melissa breathed in sharply as she looked at the paintings with renewed interest. *How could I not have noticed that before?*

It was all the same woman in the paintings, in various degrees of bondage. And the woman was her.

"They're amazing," she said truthfully.

"You're my muse."

Melissa realized that she wanted to make love to James more than anything. She would have leapt out of the bed to go to him, wrap her arms around him, if she hadn't been so tightly tethered.

After what seemed like an eternity, her nipples so taut she was sure she could cut glass with them, James finally put down his sketchbook and walked over to her. He untied her, laying her flat on the bed as he pressed his body against hers. Melissa couldn't peel his clothes off fast enough, running her hands over his muscled chest before cupping his balls in her hand.

James groaned, a low, guttural sound. He reached over to the jeans lying in a heap on the side of the bed and pulled a condom out of the pocket, quickly sheathing himself.

"I want you," Melissa whispered as he thrust himself into her, burying his cock to the hilt in one smooth motion.

He filled her completely, stroking her. The butt plug was still inside her ass, making her pussy so tight she almost felt like a virgin as he moved deeply within her.

He pounded her over and over again, eliciting moans from her that she had never experienced before. Now she knew what everyone was talking about when they mentioned the G-spot. Her orgasm was endless, melting, a slow series of spasms around his thick cock as he continued fucking her.

She moaned as the pleasure coursed through her.

"Oh…yes," she panted, barely aware that the words were coming out of her mouth even as James responded by dropping his hand between their sweaty bodies and rubbing her clit. Another orgasm racked her body and she gasped, clenching around his shaft, urging him on.

"Do you like that?" he whispered in her ear, plunging into her so hard he reached a spot up near her cervix that had her crying out her affirmation as he kept going. "'Cause I can do this all night."

Melissa wrapped her legs around his back and bucked her hips upward, meeting his thrusts with equal force, putting her on the brink of climaxing again. Suddenly his rhythm changed and he moved his torso in such a way that his lower abdomen was sliding over her slick clit, overstimulating her so much she nearly pushed against his tight pecs to get him to slow down, but he just grinned down at her and kept pace.

She couldn't speak for exhaustion as her body exploded with a sharp clitoral orgasm. His cock tightened inside her and she knew he was on the verge too.

As he came, thrusting fast, he reached behind her and pulled the plug out of her asshole in one hard motion, causing her to come again all over him.

She lay boneless on the bed, panting, as he rolled off her.

"I'm falling in love with you, you know," he said softly.

"It's crazy…but I believe you." What she didn't say was that she might be feeling the same thing.

But it was insane. It was too soon to be falling in love…and she had a lot to think about.

"So can I see you again?" James reached down to her clit and stroked it idly.

"You've got me for the rest of the weekend, right?"

He picked up the rhythm as she started to move beneath his hand.

"I want you for longer than that."

Melissa tried to push his hand away but he held firm,

flicking her clit. "Are you changing the rules of our agreement?" she asked. "You can't just blackmail me indefinitely."

He stopped playing with her pussy. "I'm no longer blackmailing you. If you want to keep the stolen Rembrandt, then you can. I won't say a word."

Melissa looked at him. "What about Hamilton? You won't tell him about this, right?"

"I lost my job over your art heist. For you. I've been working for Hamilton for years and then you pull your stunt and now I'm done."

"You got fired? Why didn't you tell me? Does this mean Hamilton knows who stole his Rembrandt?"

"Really?" James said. "That's all you can say? I tell you I was fired because of what you did and all you can think about is yourself."

"I — I'm sorry," Melissa said. "But I need to know what Hamilton is going to do."

"He can't go to the cops, obviously. And like you said, he doesn't know you were there. But he does know that I was supposed to be guarding the stairs and someone got upstairs anyway."

"What if he follows you, James, to figure out who stole his Rembrandt?"

"He might," James agreed. "And since you suddenly look like you're ready to jump out of bed, then I'm guessing the Rembrandt is more important to you than this."

"Than what?" Melissa asked, even though she knew the answer.

She had never felt this excited by any man. She could see this turning into something amazing…but she couldn't risk Hamilton finding her and stealing back the Rembrandt.

"Forget it," James said. "Forget this weekend ever happened. I'll see you around, or not. If you're so worried about losing your precious Rembrandt — "

"It *is* precious!" she exclaimed angrily.

"Yeah, I guess so. You can go home now if you'd like."

He unclipped the nipple clamps from her aching nipples and she gasped as the blood came rushing back into them. The abrupt release hurt like hell — and not just in her nipples. How could he just release *her* like that?

Melissa looked at him in shock. "So that's it? We're done?"

"If the only reason you're here is because you think I'm still blackmailing you over the Rembrandt, and you're not willing to risk losing the Rembrandt when Hamilton finds you with me, then yes. We are done."

Melissa got off the bed and pulled her clothing on hastily, cursing under her breath. *What the hell is his problem?*

CHAPTER FIVE

A few weeks later, Melissa still couldn't sleep very well. At home under her purple comforter, she felt sad and lost, as if she was in the wrong place. She *was* in the wrong place. She was supposed to be at James' house, playing with him, talking with him, falling in love with him.

Instead she was all alone in her Brooklyn brownstone, listening to her neighbors argue through the shared wall. All alone, staring at her precious stolen Rembrandt. As amazing as the painting was, it wasn't James. She had thought that having this masterpiece all to herself to enjoy would make her complete, but she would never be complete — not without the one man who had satisfied her like no other man ever could. Not without James.

So what if Hamilton found her through James? Hamilton wasn't a killer. He was an art thief — like her. She sat up in bed and grabbed her cell phone. She wasn't willing to throw away the potential of this relationship with James for a painting — not anymore.

Melissa texted him even though it was three a.m., *I miss you.*

He texted back so quickly she realized he must be as wide-awake as she was. His text said, *I'm coming over.*

Melissa sprang out of bed and quickly ran around her bedroom, straightening up. She ran a brush through her hair and splashed water on her face. Should she greet him in the sweatpants she was already wearing or change into lingerie?

Lingerie.

* * * * *

James sat on the edge of his bed, looking at his cell phone. *She missed him.* Heaven knew he missed her. He had been so hurt when it had become clear that she was not interested in him if it was at the expense of her Rembrandt. Once he had taken away the threat of blackmail, she had simply walked out his door.

He had been angry at first. So angry that he thought about kidnapping her, punishing her, forcing her to fall in love with him the way he had fallen in love with her. Instead he let her go.

It had been so hard for him to look around his bedroom and see the numerous paintings of her hanging on his walls, they just made him feel sad.

That hadn't stopped him from finishing his latest piece — the one of Melissa in nipple clamps. He had loved torturing her beautiful nipples. Was it possible he was going to get a chance to paint her again? All of his previous paintings of her had been taken from his overactive imagination. The one of her in the clamps had been drawn from life — and the painting had come out so well, he had even been able to sell it on eBay to an anonymous bidder. It was just as well, since his savings were dwindling. He'd have to find another security job soon. It wasn't as if Hamilton would ever hire him back.

But none of that mattered now. All that mattered was seeing Melissa again. Now that he was going to her house, all those original feelings of betrayal and frustration came rushing back, along with a healthy dose of relief. This wasn't over. There was still a chance for them to pursue their relationship — as long as she was willing to get rid of what she had called her "holy grail" — that damn Rembrandt.

He grabbed his duffel bag and started tossing in some of his toys, just in case she was in the mood to kiss and make up. He'd be very happy to forgive her if she was willing to prove to him that she was truly his.

James grinned as he stepped out his front door and locked it behind him, walking down the few steps of his brownstone to the sidewalk below. It would be faster to just walk the four blocks to Melissa's house than it would be to drive, since parking was a bitch in their neighborhood. The cool night air revived him. He wasn't tired, not at all.

He shouldered the duffel bag and whistled quietly to himself as he headed to see Melissa. The perfect punishment for her was already forming in his mind.

* * * * *

Melissa answered the door with a robe covering her black lacy lingerie. She was wearing a thong, as uncomfortable as it was, because she knew he loved them. Even the feel of the spandex pressed against her pussy and in her ass crack didn't bother her, knowing it was for James. There was just something about him.

James closed the door behind him and gathered her in his arms, hugging her close. The scent of clean man reminded her just how much she had missed him in the weeks after she had walked out of his house.

"I was surprised to get your text," he said.

"I just — I missed you. I'm sorry I let you think the Rembrandt is more important than you. That was stupid."

"I missed you too." James took her hand and led her up the stairs to her bedroom. "But you know I can't let you off the hook so easily."

Melissa looked at him warily. "What do you mean?"

"I want you to give Hamilton back the Rembrandt, or turn it over to the FBI."

Melissa let her robe slide off her shoulders and onto

the carpet. Maybe once James had sex on his brain he'd forget what he was asking her. James did notice her scantily clad body — she could tell by his erection — but he shook his head.

"I'm serious, Melissa."

Melissa sighed. "I know, you're right. It's just such a hard thing to imagine — letting go of this painting. Give me some time. Let me think about it."

James nodded. "You can think about it. As long as you are okay with the fact that if we are together, Hamilton will almost definitely track you down. And when he does, he will steal that painting right back."

"I understand." Melissa crossed the room to James and put her arms around his neck, kissing him deeply. They fit together so perfectly. It just seemed…right.

"I've been imagining our reunion for the past few weeks, ever since you walked out my door. You hurt me so badly, Melissa." He traced her jawline with his finger, staring into her eyes. "I want to return the favor."

Melissa smiled but there was nothing to say. It made sense that he'd need them to have a clean slate if he was going to feel comfortable opening himself up to her again.

"So — what do you think?" James asked. "May I punish you?"

Melissa felt her pussy get wet at his words, and she nodded silently. "Which of my favorite erotica scenes are you going to play out for me now?" she asked with a smile.

"Oh, this isn't anything from your books. This is a real punishment. It's not meant to be enjoyable, it's meant to prove that you are submitting to my will and that you truly belong to me."

She raised her eyebrows. *What on earth does he have in store for me?*

"So?" he pressed. "Are you still willing?"

"Yes." She'd do whatever he said, although she had to admit that she was starting to get nervous.

James looked around the room for a moment as if he

were trying to figure something out. Then he walked over to her bed and shifted the mattress and heavy box spring out of the way so that they were halfway off the bed, leaving a large gap between the mattress and the footboard.

"Come here."

She walked over to the foot of the bed, curiosity getting the better of her. The top of the footboard came up to her bellybutton. It was just a simple, wood, craftsman-style bed. The footboard had slats and a flat top piece that lay horizontally across the top, about an inch and a half wide. On the other side of the rail she could see the carpet under the bed that was normally hidden by her mattress.

"Climb on," James said. "I'll give you a hand."

"What?"

"I want you to straddle the edge of the bed."

"I — I can't reach to get on it," she said.

James grabbed several of her huge art history textbooks off the bottom shelf of her bookcase and piled a couple on each side of the bedframe. "Climb on."

Putting her feet gingerly onto the textbooks, which actually worked just fine as a makeshift step, she brought her leg up over the side of the rail at the end of the bed and sat down, straddling the footboard like a bicycle.

The thin rail pressing into her pussy was uncomfortable, and she shifted her weight to alleviate the pressure on her labia. She kept waiting for him to pull out a whip or maybe even that huge butt plug he had threatened her with that day at his house, but he seemed content to just watch her sit there.

"What's my punishment going to be?" she asked.

"To sit there until I say so," he said calmly.

"Is that all?" Melissa laughed.

That's nothing. She laughed again, relieved. She shifted her weight once more as the wood on the rail pressed against her clit. James came up to her and removed one of the books on each side that were beneath her feet.

Suddenly the pressure on her pussy increased as the rail pressed her most sensitive flesh. "Ow," she complained.

It took her a minute to realize what was happening. She stood up on her tiptoes and the pressure was immediately relieved.

"I'd like to gag you. Do I have your permission?" James asked.

Melissa smiled and nodded. "Of course. I told you, I'm yours — and I'm willing to prove it to you by doing whatever you want of me."

James pulled a ball gag out of his duffel bag and showed it to her before he popped it into her mouth. The ball filled her mouth completely, pressing her tongue down and opening her mouth so wide that she couldn't get any intelligible words out.

"Gorgeous," he said approvingly as he tightened the strap in the back. "And now I don't have to worry about you convincing me to release you from your punishment before you're truly chastised."

Melissa's pulse raced and her pussy got wet again at his words, but her calves were tiring and she had to rest them. Her heels dropped down onto the textbooks below her feet and her clit ground against the rail again, causing her to cry out against her gag.

Only a minute passed before the sensation was too intense and she put her hands down on the rail in front of her, trying to push herself up and off the pressure on her pussy.

It didn't take long before her arms got tired and she tried lifting her heels again. *Why on earth had I thought that this would be an easy punishment?*

"I can see you're really into riding this pony, aren't you?" James asked, watching her as she constantly shifted her position, rising up on her toes and then back onto her pussy, each time trying to sit on a slightly different area to keep pressure off her tender flesh.

Melissa protested against her gag as he slid the books

out completely from under her feet, causing her legs to just hang there on either side of the rail a few inches above the floor, all of her weight pressing against her clit. She rocked back and forth, trying to rise up on her hands as she tried to keep the pressure moving and not on just one spot. The sensation was so intense that she was moaning without even realizing it. She didn't think she could last much longer.

"Five minutes more and then I'll release you," James said as he came up behind her.

He held her wrists behind her back in one of his strong hands, effectively ending any chance she had of keeping all of her weight from crushing against her pussy. She squealed in surprise at the sudden pain of it, the endorphins flooding her body as she closed her eyes and tried to just give in to the sensation.

Finally he lifted her in his arms and inspected her carefully between the legs. "You don't know how much seeing that red and swollen pussy turns me on." He took the ball gag out of her mouth and kissed her lips gently. "You did great."

Melissa touched her bruised labia and inhaled sharply.

"Don't worry, you'll be fine. Now your pussy is nice and tender and ready for an orgasm," he said.

He laid her back on the skewed mattress and draped her legs over his broad shoulders. Her arm and leg muscles were so exhausted from the workout she got "riding the pony" that she couldn't have resisted even if she wanted to.

But she definitely didn't want to resist this.

He flicked his tongue out and licked her gently, tasting her, causing a sharp twinge to rush through her whole body. Her pussy was so swollen and so tender that even the lightest of flicks of his tongue brought shuddering sensation through her.

She cried out as she came once and then she nearly started crying for real when he wouldn't stop licking her clit, even though it was so overstimulated and sore that she couldn't imagine ever being able to come again. Holding her thighs spread for his relentless mouth, James brought her to orgasms two and three.

* * * * *

Melissa went to work the following afternoon to give a seminar on Egyptian art and its impact on civilization as they knew it. Even though the class was three hours long, Melissa opted to stand for the duration due to the fact that sitting was extremely uncomfortable.

The night before, James had pulled out a new paddle, one that had little cutout hearts on it. He told her he loved seeing her ass marked with hearts. But that morning when she woke up and James took a look, the hearts were gone. The only solution, he decided, was to give her a fresh spanking. She squirmed in her seat all through the drive to the college. But for some reason, she liked that constant reminder that James was in her life.

Every time she had to sit down she was forced to think of him — as if she wasn't thinking about him nonstop already.

As interesting as the subject of Egyptian art was to her, she couldn't wait to get home to see James. Her pussy was sore from riding the wooden pony as punishment last night, but she was still aching to be with him again. And not just in a physical sense — she really had missed him during their weeks apart.

Having him back in her bed last night had proven to her that she was willing to lose the Rembrandt if it meant their relationship would have a chance. He still was waiting for an answer from her about what she was going to do with the Rembrandt.

She didn't want to give it up — but for James, if it was truly that important to him, then she would. She doubted that Hamilton would give James back his job even if she returned the painting to him, so the right thing to do would be to return it to the FBI. If only she could figure out a way to do that anonymously, so she wouldn't be implicated in the theft. She wasn't about to spend the rest of her life behind bars.

Melissa had to circle her block four times before she found a parking spot. It was enough to make her want to ditch the car altogether. At least James lived close enough that they could just walk to each other's houses.

Setting her briefcase down on the front stoop of her brownstone so that she could find her house keys, Melissa realized that her door was already open.

What the hell? She pulled out her cell phone and called James.

"James, my front door is open — someone must have broken in!"

James' voice sounded calm and controlled. "Don't go inside. Just stay on your stoop and wait for the police to come check it out."

"I can't call the police, James. They'll see the Rembrandt and I'll go to prison!"

She could practically hear James thinking through the phone. "Stay where you are," he said. "I'll be right over."

It only took him a few minutes. Judging by the color in his cheeks, he had run the whole way. Melissa stood on her front stoop, her hands shaking.

James knocked loudly on the front door and then called inside, "Hello? If there's anyone in there now's your chance to get the hell out."

There was no answer. It was so quiet inside the house that Melissa could hear the ticking of the clock in the kitchen.

James looked at her and kissed her on the mouth. "I'm going in."

"I'm coming with you." Melissa said.

"No you're not. Not till I say it's safe."

James went inside while Melissa just stood there, feeling useless. Two minutes later he emerged.

"All clear."

"Is it bad in there? Is everything gone?" Melissa rushed past him to get into the house.

The TV was still there. There was even a crumpled ten-dollar bill still sitting in the bowl where she put her keys. What kind of robbery was this?

She ran upstairs. Her jewelry box was untouched on her dresser — but the Rembrandt was gone. She wailed.

"It can't be gone!"

James nodded. "It's gone all right. They left the frame, just like the original art thieves did at the museum, and just like you did when you stole it from Hamilton's."

"Hamilton. It's got to be him. He found me and he stole his painting back." She started sobbing, mourning the loss of her favorite piece of art.

"I'm sure you're right." James pulled her close and hugged her. She sobbed into his shoulder, taking comfort in his strong arms. "You knew this was a possibility if you came back to me. Now that's it actually happened, do you still think it was worth it?"

Melissa looked at the empty frame hanging on her wall and then into James' beautiful green eyes.

"Absolutely. It's worth it."

James laughed and kissed her. "You know what? We'll wait until Hamilton lets his guard down — say, one year from now? And we'll steal it back for you, Melissa. I promise."

Melissa smiled. She loved that not only was he willing to risk stealing the painting back for her, but he was planning on being with her in a year's time.

"That sounds great."

"How was work today?" he asked.

"Good. Just couldn't sit down."

James grinned and unzipped her skirt, tugging it down. "It'll be even harder to sit down tomorrow with the butt plug in your ass."

"No way in hell," she said, smiling, already feeling better even though her painting had been stolen. "I'll just take it out as soon as I get to work."

"We'll see about that, smarty pants."

CHAPTER SIX

One Year Later

Melissa watched James as he sat at his kitchen table, taking notes and talking details and contracts. James had a devilish twinkle in his eye when he got off the phone.

"What? Why are you looking at me like that?" Melissa asked, laughing.

"We're in," James said.

Melissa whooped with delight. "Oh my gosh. This is it." She knew without asking that he must have been on the phone with Hamilton's people. They had been waiting for this opportunity for months. "Who're you sending in for the job?"

James picked up his PDA and started scrolling through it. "Not Bailey. Not Holmes. Not Jackson. Reynolds is our guy. He owes me one for hiring him in the first place, and I've known him since high school."

James' private security company had been doing pretty well in the past year since its inception. James took guys on, trained them, and then hired them out for events and longer-term security assignments. He took a cut off the top for securing them a job and then paid his men as private contractors. He was making so much money that he wasn't even working security himself anymore.

Melissa had known it was only a matter of time before the good word of mouth about James' security agency got back to Hamilton. Especially since James headhunted all of the best private security specialists in the city to fill his roster.

Now they had a man on the inside.

* * * * *

There must have been over two hundred people at Hamilton's granddaughter's wedding. Melissa thought it was a lovely idea for the bride and groom to take their vows in their grandparents' sprawling, impeccably manicured garden.

Melissa had learned an important lesson about crashing parties. The people who were most likely to go unnoticed were the hired help. Everyone was wearing a uniform, so she wasn't easily identifiable. The guests barely looked at her, much less tried to engage her in conversation. And this way, she could wear sensible flats. Pretending to be with the catering crew was so much easier than pretending to mix among Hamilton's moneyed friends.

Melissa took a deep breath and tried to speak softly without moving her lips. "I'm here," she said into her Bluetooth earpiece.

It was nice knowing that James was sitting in his car just a few blocks away, and having his voice in her ear for encouragement.

"Go to the back door where the servants enter," he reminded her. His voice came through loud and clear on her tiny earpiece.

She walked around to the back, glancing nervously over her shoulder. *Does anyone recognize me?*

James' man Reynolds let her in through the back door. Melissa knew that Reynolds was risking his job by participating in the art heist, but James had assured him that he would be able to get him other security jobs if he was caught or fired.

"I'm in," she whispered.

"Good job," James said in her earpiece. "Go upstairs. Reynolds will keep watch at the bottom."

Melissa carried a large cardboard box that was supposed to contain food to be set out on platters, but instead contained…nothing. Her pulse quickened with anticipation as she ascended the main stairs. Third door on the right.

"I'm at the door," she said, her voice barely above a whisper. She turned the handle, but the door wouldn't budge. "Damn."

"Is it locked?" James asked.

"Yes." She'd had a feeling the door to Hamilton's private gallery would be locked after what had happened last year, when *she* had stolen his most prized possession. How could it not be?

"Take your time," James' voice urged in her earpiece. "You can do this. Now's when all your practice pays off."

Melissa set the cardboard box down and pulled out her tools. She kept looking over her shoulder, worried that someone would come upon her and see her picking the lock on the door. There would be no way to explain that away.

The lock wasn't easy to pick, but James had made her practice often in the past month, even having her pick a lock while he did all sorts of devious things to distract her. He had pinched her nipples, and when she started to tune that distraction out he switched to pinching her clit. That, she had to admit, had been pretty hard to ignore as she worked on the lock. But for every extra second it took her to pick the practice lock, James added an extra smack with the paddle to her nightly maintenance spanking, so she had been motivated. James said it would make it easier to pick a lock under stress in a real-world situation. Amazingly, he was right.

She listened for the telltale *click* of the lock and then

she was in.

Melissa stepped inside and switched on the light. There was a painting on the wall, but it wasn't the Rembrandt. It was a painting of her. She recognized James' style — his bold brushstrokes and the subdued, almost monochromatic colors — but this painting hadn't come from James' bedroom. It must have been a painting he did based on the sketch of her in bondage with the nipple clamps. In the painting, her brown curls cascaded down over her back as her breasts arched forward, the thin silver chain hanging down between her erect nipples.

"James! Remember when you told me you sold one of your pieces?"

"Yeah?"

"It's here. In Hamilton's gallery."

She could hear James let out a low sigh. "I can't believe this," he said.

Melissa just stood in front of the painting of herself in bondage, dumbstruck. She could tell that to James, she was a woman to be cherished. She loved looking at herself through his eyes. She loved James.

The thought stopped her in her tracks, and her eyes flitted over the paintings before her without really seeing them. She loved James. Completely and thoroughly. Why had it taken her so long to admit that one truth to herself?

"James?" she whispered.

"Melissa, this is how he found you and the Rembrandt," James said, his voice low and urgent. "I should have known he'd find us — Hamilton always does his homework on new artists. He traced you through my painting."

Wait a minute. The Rembrandt. *The Storm on the Sea of Galilee* was there, hanging in a frame on the opposite wall. Breaking into a huge smile, Melissa set her cardboard box down.

"It's here, James. The Rembrandt."

"No — Melissa. It's a trap. Get out of there now."

"I can't just leave my Rembrandt here, James," she hissed. "I'm taking it."

Stepping forward resolutely, Melissa made quick work of separating the canvas from the frame. She rolled it carefully and put it in the box. "We're good to go."

"Finally," James said. "Get the hell out of there before you get caught."

Melissa practically ran out of the gallery and down the stairs, nodding discreetly to Reynolds as she passed him.

No one even noticed that one of the caterers had taken a large box, put it in her car, and driven off before the reception even began. And none of the security guards, when questioned by Mr. Hamilton the following day, had seen a thing.

* * * * *

Melissa lay wrapped in the sheet, looking across her bedroom to her Rembrandt. It still brought a smile to her face every time she looked at it, which had been pretty much constantly since she had brought it back home last week.

James walked back into the bedroom dripping wet from his shower and Melissa shrieked as he lay down next to her and pressed his cold body against hers, getting her all wet.

"Not fair," she said.

James ignored her and nuzzled his wet face against her neck, sending chills down her spine.

"I like to air-dry," he said as he licked little circles against her pulse, gently nipping the skin with his lips.

All of Melissa's annoyance at getting wet was gone in an instant as she felt his hand sneak up under the covers and caress her breast. He tweaked her nipple, rolling it between his fingers until she moaned. It felt amazing. Her nipples had gotten so sensitive from all of the things James liked to do them. It was almost as if he kept her whole body in a state of hyperawareness.

Melissa lay back on her pillow and sighed. "I'm so glad

we got the Rembrandt back again."

"For now."

"For now," Melissa agreed. Hamilton would probably steal it back one day. And then she'd have to steal it back from him. They could play that game forever until they both decided it was time to hand the painting over to the FBI. It would have to be done carefully, anonymously. She could never just turn herself in to the FBI.

"James," she said, "where is this going?"

James continued playing with her nipple. "Well, first I was thinking I'd take some clothespins, and then — "

"No, not what you're doing with my breasts — I was actually talking about us. Where are *we* going?"

James grinned. "I was wondering when you would bring that up."

Melissa frowned. "What are you talking about?"

"I've been crazy about you since I first met you. I turned my life upside down so that I could blackmail you into getting to know me. I've put my company's reputation on the line to help you steal a priceless painting — "

"Which I appreciate," she said.

James flicked her nipple with his fingers. "Don't interrupt."

"Sorry."

"I've painted you, over and over again, because you are my muse," he continued. "In case you haven't noticed, I'm in love with you, Melissa."

Melissa couldn't help smiling, but she didn't interrupt this time.

"I know that despite the way our relationship is," he said, shrugging his shoulder in the general direction of the pile of silk cords that lay in a heap on the carpet near the bed, "or perhaps because of it, there are certain key aspects where it would be important for you to call the shots."

"Like us moving in together?" Melissa asked, squealing as James rolled her over and spanked her playfully for interrupting again.

"I don't want to just live together, Melissa," he said, rolling her back so that she gazed up at him. "I love you. I want to marry you."

"I love you too," she said.

It felt so natural, so right to say it. Why had she held back for so long?

"Will you marry me?" James asked.

"Of course I'll marry you," she said, sitting up and throwing her arms around his neck. "Were you really waiting all this time until I got around to bringing up our future?"

"I've made numerous hints about where this was going, but you never seemed too keen on exploring what that meant. I want you to know that just because we get married, maybe have kids someday, doesn't mean that we have to be all *Leave It to Beaver*. We can still have our special kind of relationship."

"That sounds good," Melissa said. "I should have told you how I felt — but I didn't fully figure it out until I saw that painting you did of me hanging on Hamilton's wall."

"But it's not like the time was wasted, you know," James said, standing up, still naked from his shower. "It gave me time to buy you this." He walked over to his pants pocket and pulled out a ring box.

"Oh my gosh. Is that what I think it is?"

James got down on one knee and opened the box. Inside, nestled in blue velvet, lay a simple one-carat princess-cut diamond set in white gold. It was gorgeous.

"How long have you been carrying around that ring?" Melissa asked.

"Um, I bought this shortly after you rode the wooden pony for me. I knew then that you were meant to be mine."

"But that was only a few weeks after we got together."

"What can I say? I love you. I'll love you forever." James took the ring out of the box. He took her left hand gently in his as he slipped the ring on her finger.

"I'll love you forever too, James," she said, smiling as he pressed his lips against hers.

"So we're engaged now," James said.

"We are."

"We have to celebrate," he said, circling his hands around her wrists and drawing them up above her head.

Melissa wrapped her legs around his muscular back and arched herself against him as he thrust inside her with one long stroke. Gasping as his cock beat mercilessly against that certain spot deep inside her that made her melt, Melissa kissed his neck and held on for the ride.

The End

Author's Note

Rembrandt's *The Storm on the Sea of Galilee* is still missing to this day. If you have any information concerning this painting or the circumstances of this crime, you can submit a tip online to the FBI.

Since the original publication of *Punishing the Art Thief* in 2010, the FBI has begun offering a five million dollar reward for its return.

ABOUT
SHOSHANNA EVERS

New York Times and *USA Today* bestselling author
Shoshanna Evers grew up in New York and also lived in
Florida and Los Angeles before settling with her family
and three big dogs in northern Idaho, where inspiration
abounds, and Shoshanna can't help but see everything
through the eyes of a city girl.

She has written dozens of sexy stories. Shoshanna
Evers is best known for The Tycoon's Convenient
Bride...and Baby, The Enslaved Trilogy, Overheated, and
How to Write Hot Sex, among others. Her work has been
featured in *Best Bondage Erotica 2012* and *Best Bondage Erotica
2013*, the Penguin/Berkley Heat anthology *Agony/Ecstasy*,
and in numerous other anthologies.

Punishing the Art Thief was originally published in 2010
by Ellora's Cave Publishing. This book was Shoshanna's
very first published work. The edition you're reading has
been slightly updated for 2015, including the new cover
art.

Reviewers have called Shoshanna's writing "sensuous,
delightful, and sizzling" with stories where "the plot is
fresh and the pacing excellent, the emotions…real and
poignant."

Shoshanna used to work as a syndicated advice
columnist and a registered nurse, but now she's a full-time

smut writer and a home-schooling mom. Evers is also the cofounder of SelfPubBookCovers.com, the largest selection of instantly customizable premade book covers in the world.

She loves to connect with readers!

Sexily *Evers* After...

Want to know when my next book comes out?
Sign up for my newsletter to hear about new releases first, and read excerpts you won't find in the sample pages!
ShoshannaEvers.com/newsletter

"I liked this book, what should I read next?"
Thanks! Check out Chastity Belt, The Enslaved Trilogy (start with Enslaved, Book 1 in the Enslaved Trilogy), Ginger Snap, and the Becoming Hers Trilogy for more BDSM erotic romance. Want less kink, more romance? Check out The Tycoon's Convenient Bride...and Baby, or I Am Not Your Melody. Or type my name into any search bar at your retailer of choice, and happy reading!

****To my readers:
If you enjoyed this book, I'd love if you could leave an honest review! Reviews are so important; thank you for taking the time — I really appreciate it!

Visit **ShoshannaEvers.com**
for monthly giveaways and red-hot excerpts!

Let's be BFF's!
Twitter @ShoshannaEvers
Facebook/shoshanna.evers

A RED-HOT TRILOGY BY

Shoshanna
EVERS

An erotic romp across the playgrounds of
the unbelievably rich and extremely sexy

DOWNLOAD YOUR COPIES TODAY!

www.ingramcontent.com/pod-product-compliance
Lightning Source LLC
Chambersburg PA
CBHW020312150626
46552CB00022B/2839